# Nathaniel McDaniel
## AND THE
## Magic Attic

# The Sabre-toothed Tiger

BY Evan Solomon

ILLUSTRATED BY Bill Slavin

PUFFIN
CANADA

*Acknowledgments*

Nate and Tut never leave the attic without the genius of Bill Slavin; the devoted support of Barbara Berson and Tracy Bordian; the team at Penguin Canada, including Karen McMullin and Mary Opper; Michael Levine and Maxine Quigley; the folks at D Code; the Solomon and Quinn clans, with new addition Thomas; Yolly Angeles; and Virginia, whose famed "Pete" stories sparked the whole voyage. But as Nate and Tut always say, the real magic behind any journey is found with Tammy, Maizie, and Gideon and, yes, our little cat, Shasha.

---

PUFFIN CANADA
Published by the Penguin Group

Penguin Group (Canada), 90 Eglinton Avenue East, Suite 700, Toronto, Ontario, Canada M4P 2Y3 (a division of Pearson Canada Inc.)

Penguin Group (USA) Inc., 375 Hudson Street, New York, New York 10014, U.S.A.
Penguin Books Ltd, 80 Strand, London WC2R 0RL, England
Penguin Ireland, 25 St Stephen's Green, Dublin 2, Ireland (a division of Penguin Books Ltd)
Penguin Group (Australia), 250 Camberwell Road, Camberwell, Victoria 3124, Australia
 (a division of Pearson Australia Group Pty Ltd)
Penguin Books India Pvt Ltd, 11 Community Centre, Panchsheel Park, New Delhi – 110 017, India
Penguin Group (NZ), cnr Airborne and Rosedale Roads, Albany, Auckland 1310, New Zealand
 (a division of Pearson New Zealand Ltd)
Penguin Books (South Africa) (Pty) Ltd, 24 Sturdee Avenue, Rosebank, Johannesburg 2196,
 South Africa

Penguin Books Ltd, Registered Offices: 80 Strand, London WC2R 0RL, England

First published 2007                    1 2 3 4 5 6 7 8 9 10

Text copyright © Evan Solomon, 2007     Illustrations copyright © Bill Slavin, 2007

ISBN-10: 0-670-06387-8                   ISBN-13: 978-0-670-06387-1

Manufactured in Asia

Visit the Penguin Group (Canada) website at **www.penguin.ca**

Special and corporate bulk purchase rates available; please see **www.penguin.ca/corporatesales** or call 1-800-810-3104, ext. 477 or 474

For my son Gideon, who makes
every day a miraculous adventure
— E.S.

For Owyn
— B.S.

Nathaniel McDaniel loves to explore.
He peeks into dressers and opens closed doors.
His big eyes are green, his shoes need repair,
and he *never* combs his straw-coloured hair.

Every Sunday Nate sees his Gramps,
it's just automatic...

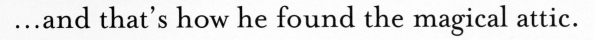

# ...and that's how he found the magical attic.

A place full of artifacts, relics, and antiques,
it has a smoky aroma and a curious mystique.
There are masks from the Mayans
and a gunpowder bowl, a telescope,
a periscope, and a totem pole.

But any relic Nate touches takes
him through time and through space;
he can't come home till it's returned
to its proper place.

Now if you remember the pirates
Nate survived last week, you'll understand
why he's changing his exploring technique.
Today Nate's bringing something on
which to depend: not a sword, not a shield,
but a trustworthy *friend*.

It's his Gramps' golden cat who
likes to prowl, snoop, and strut.
She follows Nate's trail, and
her name is Queen Tut.
She's clever and loyal, and
gives good advice; she prefers
**peanut butter cookies**
to the sour taste
of mice.

So with Tut at his side and no adult's permission, Nate marches off on his next expedition. Arriving at the attic, Nate lets the key slide:

one *click*, one *clack*,

and they're on *the inside*.

Creeping past the mummy,
and some swords in a bin,
Tut bolts straight ahead for a
woolly mammoth's skin.

"Be careful!" cries Nate.
"Don't touch that hide!
That mammoth's gonna take you
on a really weird ride."

But it's too late to stop her—Tut
settles down on the fur.
She licks her paws, and her claws,
and then starts to *purr*.

# BA-ZANG

goes the magic.

# BA-ZING

it jump-starts. Nate leaps onto the pelt just before Tut departs. They spin and they tumble on a purple airwave, and with a BLAST and a BUMP they land in…

"Are you all right?"
　Nate asks his feline companion,
　　because Tut looks like she's
　　just been shot from a cannon.
　　Her hair puffs and it fuzzes,
　　　she gives a burp and a sneeze,
　she wobbles and bobbles on
　　all four of her knees.

"I'm not sure where we are,
　　even where we should start,
but take a look around, Tut,
　　at all the really strange art."

On the cave walls they see
　　paintings of bison and birds,
　　and men out hunting
　　enormous elk herds.

Suddenly a drumbeat starts
　　to pound and to grow,
　louder, then louder with
　　a booming echo.

"T-Tut," Nate whispers,
　　as the cat pricks up her ears,
　"we've gone back in time
*more than a hundred thousand years.*"

Still, there's no use in crying, complaining, or despairing,
a good explorer always starts by finding his bearings.
Scrambling on top of some moss-covered boulders,
Nate pulls the mammoth coat up over his shoulders.

In the distance lights flicker, and Nate smells smoke in the air,
so he jumps down to consult with his faithful confrere.
But Tut is too curious to sit around and wait,
and she darts on ahead to investigate.

"Wait up!" calls Nate, scurrying to keep up to her pace,
when rounding a corner he comes upon a startling place.

His jaw falls...

his breathing stalls...

right in front of Nate there's a riot of...

They have thick hairy brows
    and protruding lower jaws;
their long fingernails
    look like animal claws.
    Some are scratching,
    some stomping,
    some waving flint spears;
some dress as rhinos and
some as reindeers.

"Tut, where are you?"
    Nate wonders, getting frantic,
when behind him springs
    a man who's *bigger*
        than gigantic.

    "WHO YOU?"
    bellows the Giant with
        eyes full of hate.
    Nathaniel turns to run,
    but it's far too late.
    Snatching Nate up,
    mammoth skin and all,
    the Giant holds him
        in the air like a
        human football.

The drumming falls silent, the crowd closes in,
   dirty hands reach out to poke at Nate's trembling skin.
Someone pinches his arm; another tugs at his clothes.
   The Reindeer Man sniffs at him with
      his bulbous black nose.

"Pum in tum!" rumbles the Giant, pointing to Nate. He smacks his lips and starts to salivate. "Pum in tum!" the others repeat in delight, rubbing their stomachs with appetite.

Nate struggles, he squirms, he refuses to quit, but the Giant ties him tightly to a boar-roasting spit.

With a heave and a lift he sets Nate over the fire,
and the flames beneath him rise higher and higher.
The cave dwellers dance; they shout in a fury.
They want Nate cooked to perfection then spiced in a curry.

"It's over," Nate thinks,

"I'm done, gone, deceased," when suddenly

the Giant screams out…

The crowd gasps and gawps, and points to the wall,
where the shadow of a tiger looms twenty feet tall.
Quick as rabbits they exit; they bolt, scatter, and flee.
Some head for the river, while the Giant climbs a tree.

Left alone is poor Nate, hanging above those hot flames,
waiting for a tiger to pick at his remains.
Just as he bids the world *au revoir, goodbye, ciao…*

…he hears Tut sing out her
distinctive *Meee-ow!*
From the darkness Tut emerges
—that courageous furball—
it was *her* shadow cast
way up there on the wall.

"They thought you were a tiger!"
Nate calls out with relief.
"Now untie me before I turn
into a side of roast beef."

Gnashing and scratching,
Tut severs the twine.
Nate escapes from the fire
thanks to his faithful feline.
But the mammoth hide
on Nate's shoulders,
which he has to return,
got crisped in the fire and
now has a burn.

Who does it belong to and where should they look?
With time-travel exploring there's no guidebook.
Nate must be home by six-thirty—there's no time to rest—
so they leave the cave quickly for…

There are crocodiles, wildebeests,
and horned lizards eating mice.
Poison plants, fire ants
—it's a deadly paradise.
They pass boas wrapped 'round branches
and spiders big as backpacks.

They see vicious rats,

vampire bats,

and then…

sabre-tooth tracks!

A shriek interrupts them and vultures burst
into the sky. In front of Nate trees rustle,
catching his eye.

"Don't move, Tut," Nate orders
with a feeling of dread.
"Something enormous
is coming at us,
dead ahead!"

# CRASH

comes a woolly mammoth, who is anything but small,
and he has no fur on him—no, *no fur at all!*
His tusks are ivory white and his skin is maroon.
He looks like a shrivelled-up, ten-tonne prune.

Striding past Tut, the mammoth heads straight for Nate.
The beast can move pretty quickly considering his weight.
Bending his head down, his great eyes open wide,
"Hey kid," the mammoth asks,

"Is that really my hide?"

Nathaniel McDaniel can't believe what he's heard.
An animal who speaks English … that's completely absurd!

"Don't go runnin' off," says the mammoth.
"I'm harmless, I swear. The name's Woolly Ed,
 and all I want is my hair."

"You can talk?" Nate gasps, still in utter disbelief.
"Let me explain," says Ed. "And I'll keep it brief.
 It's a talent that makes my species both rare and distinct,
 but so much talking has made us almost completely extinct.
 You see, as my family sits around enjoying a pleasant
 evening chat, we forget that we're being stalked by
 a sabre-toothed cat."

Nate's curiosity is buzzing, and he doesn't mean to be rude,
but he's gotta ask why Ed's walking 'round in the nude.

"The tiger did that, too." Ed turns red with shame.
"And since I lost my hide things just haven't been the same.
It happened when I went out walking to visit a sick friend,
who lives near the river, just 'round the bend.
All at once there was a roar, and Sabre launched an attack.
Within seconds he'd leapt up onto my thick, hairy back.
But before that scoundrel could sink his fangs in too deep,
my hide slid to the ground in one sloppy heap.
He still tried to catch me and gobble me up,
but I ran away naked as a newborn pup. Since then
I've been freezing—a mammoth
needs his coat—and I miss
my hair so badly that
I've become quite remote."

Hearing the woeful tale, Nate wipes away a tear,
and even Tut gets choked up by the sad atmosphere.
Moving over to Ed, who's now too upset to speak,
Tut gives him a soft lick on his blubbery cheek.

"I'm sorry about everything," says Nate. "Please don't despair.
After all, we've brought you back your natural hair."

But before Nate can return Ed's long-lost fur,
the moment is destroyed by...

Out marches a tiger fierce
as a samurai, with two deadly
incisors and a glowing red eye.
Sabre's claws are like scalpels
and so is each fang. They can
cut through flesh and bone
like lemon meringue.

Sabre lunges for Ed, who has little time for reaction,
and Nate knows he must create an instant distraction.
So he holds up Ed's coat like a matador's cape,
waving it like he'd seen once on a videotape.

The move draws Sabre's attention, so he
turns toward Nate. He has a nasty look that says,
"There's room for two on my plate."

Charging wildly, Sabre slashes his fangs in a fray,
but at the very last second Nate moves out of the way.
Again Sabre attacks, then *three times more*,
and each time Nate escapes like a toreador.

With a snarl and a hiss Sabre stares down his prey
while Nate jiggles Ed's hide and calls out, "Olé!"

But Nate's arms are getting tired, he can't do this much longer,
and it looks like the tiger is only getting stronger.
In a flash Nate has an idea, though it's no guarantee:
what if he waves the fur right in front of a tree?

Sabre leaps like a missile, his teeth on the mark,
but Nate pulls away the hide and Sabre bites into the bark.
SNAP! goes one incisor and POP! goes the other.
Sabre's fangs drop to the ground, one after another.

"It worked!" yells Nate, punching a fist in the air.
"That tiger is no match for Woolly Ed's hair!"

Sabre teeters, totters, almost trips on his claws.
He sticks out his tongue to feel his now toothless jaws.
Then he slinks off to the forest and Ed trumpets a blast,
"We're free of that menace. We're free at last!"

The time has now come for Nate to return Ed's shag,
which saved them all from that prehistoric scalawag.

"It got singed in delivery," Nate explains with
a shrug, but Ed just wraps him up in
a mammoth-trunk hug.

Then Nate spreads out the fur and without
another word said, he flings it high
over the back of his pal Big Woolly Ed.

At that moment Nate and Tut start to sway and to stumble.
Everything around them begins to pitch and to rumble.
They wave goodbye to Ed as he settles into his hair—
he's so much happier in his all-season wear.
Then they shut their eyes tightly and hear some loud static, and

# BA-ZANG!

### and BA-ZING!

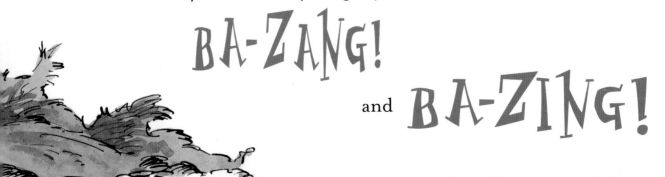

...they're back home in the attic.

There's no time to sit back and recuperate.
Nate's parents will be coming and he can't make them wait.
They run from the attic and lock up the door, hiding the key
carefully 'cause they'll be back for some more.

Nate bounds down the stairs, Tut close at his heel,
and there's his Gramps waiting, holding a box with a seal.

"Nathaniel, where were you?" Gramps asks with a wink.

"I've got a very special present. You'll like it, I think."

Then he opens his case and makes a selection. He gives Nate a stamp straight from his collection. Nate tries to say thanks, but he can only stand and stare, for the stamp shows Woolly Ed, all covered with hair.

Nate gazes at his Gramps, who is truly a mystery.

He's a man whose life spans all time and all history.

Holding the stamp carefully (it's a very rare antique),

## Nate promises his Gramps…

…he'll be back
next week.